MOEBIUS®

# MADWOMAN™
## OF THE SACRED HEART
JODOROWSKY

STORY BY ALEXANDRO JODOROWSKY
ART BY JEAN "MOEBIUS" GIRAUD

*Letters by Dave Cooper*

DARK · HORSE
· COMICS ·®

# MADWOMAN OF THE SACRED HEART™

**RANDY & JEAN-MARC LOFFICIER**
*translators and editors for Starwatcher Graphies*

**SCOTT ALLIE, EDWARD MARTIN III,
& RANDY STRADLEY**
*editors*

**MARK COX & JULIE GASSAWAY**
*designers*

Mike Richardson • publisher
Neil Hankerson • executive vice president
David Scroggy • vice president of publishing
Lou Bank • vice president of sales & marketing
Andy Karabatsos • vice president of finance
Mark Anderson • general counsel
Randy Stradley • creative director

Cindy Marks • director of production & design
Mark Cox • art director
Sean Tierney • computer graphics director
Michael Martens • director of sales
Tod Borleske • director of licensing
Mark Ellington • director of operations
Dale LaFountain • director of m.i.s.

Published by
Dark Horse Comics, Inc.
10956 SE Main St.
Milwaukie, OR 97222

August 1996
First edition
ISBN 1-56971-136-4

2 4 6 8 10 9 7 5 3 1

# F O R E W O R D

Confrontations with the central symbols of the Christian faith are something generally avoided by authors of science (or speculative) fiction. Partly out of literary cowardice, obviously, but also because the concept of Christ the Savior is so fundamentally ingrained in our western culture that few writers can step far enough away to cast a new light on it.

Michael Moorcock's remarkable *Behold the Man* (1966, expanded into novel form in 1969), itself a hugely controversial work, uses the device of time travel to enable its hero, Karl Glogauer, to suffer crucifixion and become Christ in his search for his own redemption. (Another interesting, although lesser-known variant on the same theme is Barry Malzberg's 1982 *Cross of Fire*.)

But that's it for Christ in science fiction. Yes, there are a few other stories—such as James Blish's Hugo Award-winning *A Case of Conscience* (1958), Walter M. Miller's Hugo Award-winning *A Canticle for Leibowitz* (1960) (notice the pattern?), or, more recently, Philip José Farmer's *Jesus on Mars* (1979)— dealing with Christian issues, but they always do it through the safe filter of time and alien societies, certainly not in actual, meaningful, possibly blasphemous fashion.

The fact that, in the entire body of speculative fiction, one can only find two works challenging the very essence of the Christian faith is, in and of itself, interesting. It takes a very astute fish to not only divine the presence of water but to analyze it.

This is what makes Alexandro Jodorowsky's *Madwoman of the Sacred Heart* so unique, so different, and ultimately so rewarding. In a field where *different* has come to mean a change in the color of one's tights, Jodorowsky is not afraid to take the Scriptures at face value and ask the $64,000 question: If God, the God of the Bible, acting on ancient covenants, decided to send another son, a new Messiah, to earth today, what then?

What then, indeed?

In a world of narco-terrorism, fifty-second soundbites, and multi-national corporations, how would we deal with a new Savior? Would we, like the Romans, even be aware of the birth of the new Messiah? Could we tell the difference between John the Baptist and just another sect of nuts? Where does the line lie between faith and sanity? Between miracles and coincidences?

Jodorowsky's skill is that he never stacks the deck in favor of either alternative. He does not offer any easy, pre-packaged answers. The reader is ultimately free to decide if the faithful are madmen or illuminati.

One man who appears to have made up his mind is the artist—Moebius—who counterpoints Jodorowsky's story well with a dynamic, nervous look, often verging on an editorial-cartoon style. Indeed, Moebius gave the protagonist, Professor Mangel, Jodorowsky's own likeness, a telling, even subversive, editorial comment.

**Randy & Jean-Marc Lofficier**

# CHAPTER
# ONE

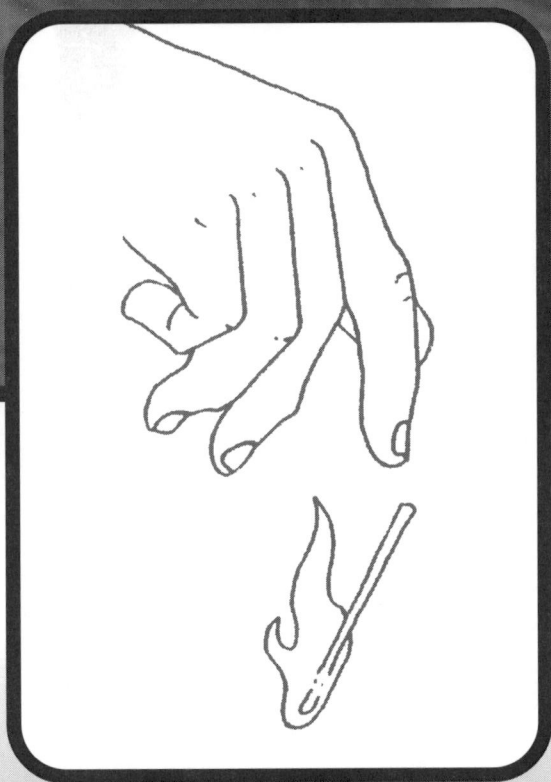

LISTEN UP! BEFORE YOU CUT THE CAKE, I'VE GOT A BIG SURPRISE HERE FOR MY HUSBAND!
IT'S YOUR BIRTH-DAY PRESENT, ALAN!
OH, MYRA, I'M REALLY TOUCHED!
BUT... THEY'RE DIVORCE PAPERS!
DIVORCE?
WHAT?
I... I DIDN'T EXPECT THIS...
IS THIS A JOKE?
THE PROFESSOR HAS DONE NOTHING TO DE-SERVE SUCH A SCENE!
I ALWAYS KNEW IT!
C'MON! IT'S NOT THE END OF THE WORLD! ALAN SHOULD BE HAPPY. IF HE JUST SIGNS THESE PAPERS, HE'LL BE FREE OF ME!
HE'S NEVER LEFT ANY OF HIS WIVES. HE JUST BE-HAVES IN A WAY TO MAKE US LEAVE HIM. I'M HIS THIRD WIFE...
...AND THE THIRD ONE TO DO THIS! ACCORDING TO HIS OWN THEORIES OF NON-ACTION, HE CAN'T BRING HIMSELF TO THROW AWAY A LEMON, EVEN WHEN HE'S SQUEEZED EVERY LAST DROP OUT OF IT. INSTEAD, HE JUST OPENS HIS FINGERS AND GENTLY RELEASES THE FRUIT, WHICH FALLS BY ITSELF, THANKS TO THE LAW OF GRAVITY!
THIS IS GOING TO GET NASTY...
MAYBE WE SHOULD GO?
BUT SURELY...
JODO. MOEB. 5

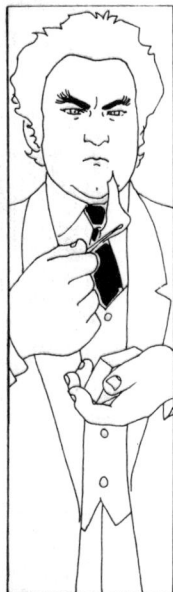

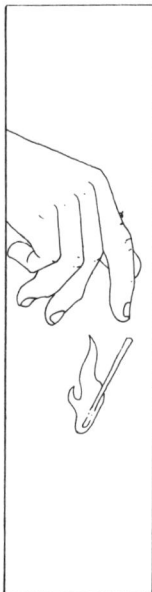

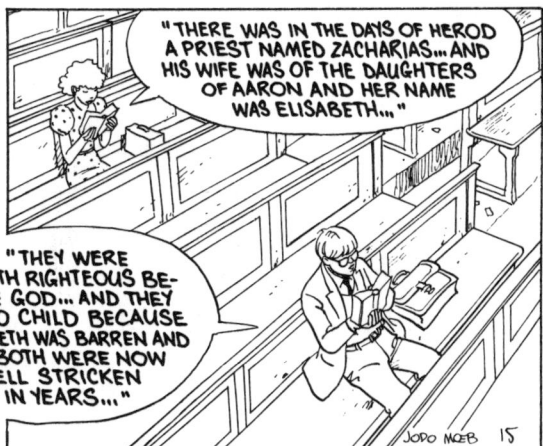

"AND THERE APPEARED UNTO HIM AN ANGEL OF THE LORD ...THY WIFE ELISABETH SHALL BEAR THEE A SON, AND THOU SHALT CALL HIS NAME **JOHN**... HE SHALL BE GREAT IN THE SIGHT OF THE LORD... AND HE SHALL BE FILLED WITH THE HOLY GHOST, EVEN FROM HIS MOTHER'S WOMB, AND MANY OF THE CHILDREN OF ISRAEL SHALL HE TURN TO THE LORD THEIR GOD..."

"AND IT CAME TO PASS THAT AS SOON AS THE DAYS OF HIS MINISTRATION WERE ACCOMPLISHED, HE DEPARTED TO HIS OWN HOUSE...AND AFTER THOSE DAYS, HIS WIFE ELISABETH CONCEIVED..."

AFTER "HE DEPARTS TO HIS OWN HOUSE," LUKE DEPRIVES US OF THE DESCRIPTION OF THE MOST BEAUTIFUL ACT OF LOVE EVER KNOWN TO MANKIND...

"THE ANCIENT HOLY MAN RETURNED HOME, PAINFULLY CROSSING THE PARCHED LAND...

"BUT ALTHOUGH ALL THINGS ARE THE SAME, NOTHING IS LIKE ANY OTHER THING IN THIS WORLD...

"THE EARTH BEGAN TO SHAKE LIKE A RUTTING BEAST. THE CLOUDS OF DUST BECAME LIKE UNTO INEBRIATED BUTTERFLIES...

"A BURNING WIND IMPLANTED THE DIVINE DECREE OF COPULATION IN THE HEARTS OF BEAST AND HERB...

MOEBIORO 16

"THE STRENGTH OF LOVE RATTLED THE VERY NATURE... AN IMMENSE JOY MADE ZACHARIAS DANCE AND PRANCE, HIS ANCIENT FLESH FOLLOWING THE DEMANDS OF HIS REJUVENATED DESIRE..."

"ZACHARIAS AND ELISABETH, WHO HAD LIVED TOGETHER ALL THEIR LIVES, FINALLY MET FOR THE FIRST TIME, INHABITED BY THE HOLY GHOST..."

"AND THESE TWO FIERY SPIRITS, OVERTAKEN BY AN APOCALYPTIC DESIRE, SOUGHT EACH OTHER AND MERGED THEIR WITHERED FLESH..."

JODO-MŒBIUS 17

"AND THOSE TWO DECAYING BODIES, POSSESSED BY THE LUST OF THE HOLY GHOST, RADIATED AN ASTONISHING BEAUTY. IT IS FROM THE MIRACLE OF THIS ACT THAT JOHN THE BAPTIST WAS BORN. THE MOST BEAUTIFUL OF ALL MEN, THE CHILD BORN OF DIVINE PASSION, THE FUTURE HERALD OF THE COMING OF COSMIC CONSCIOUSNESS!"

TO REACH THE CHRIST WITHIN US, IT IS NECESSARY TO FIRST GO THROUGH JOHN. IF WE DO NOT HARBOR A HOLY WILL, WORK HARD ON THE GIFT OF ONESELF, THEN WE SHALL NEVER ACCOMPLISH THE BIRTH OF OUR INNER GOD!

MY CHILDREN, THERE IS NO OTHER WAY BUT LOVE!

OOoooH!

CLAP CLAP CLAP

SORRY ABOUT BEING SUCH AN IN-CONVENIENCE, ELISABETH!

BUT IT'S A GREAT HONOR, PROFESSOR!

MOEB, JODO.

18

YOU COULD HAVE CRUSHED HER FACE UNDER YOUR RAGING FIST WITH THE FURY OF A SCREAM TORN FROM YOUR BALLS!
NO! PLEASE, NO!
AND FOAMING WITH DESIRE, YOU COULD HAVE BEATEN HER SENSELESS!
AND TORN OFF HER BLOODIED CLOTHES PIECE BY PIECE, THE WAY YOU WOULD SKIN A SACRIFICIAL LAMB!
WHAT AN ABOMINATION! HOW CAN I STILL NURTURE SUCH POISON IN MY SOUL?
YOU COULD HAVE REAMED HER VAGINA AND HER ANUS AND BURIED YOURSELF DEEP WITHIN HER, MAKING HER SPEW HER ORGASMS LIKE THE SLOBBERING BITCH SHE IS! YOU COULD HAVE...
ENOUGH! ENOUGH!
RAAHHHHHHH
JODO.MOEB
25

JODO MOEB. 31

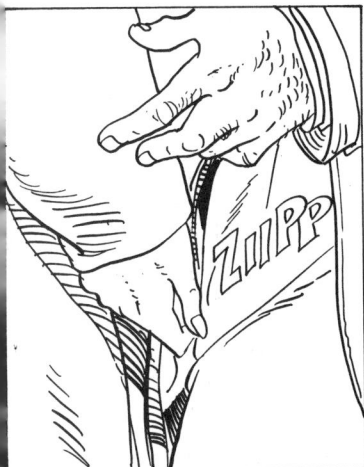

"EIGHT YEARS AGO, MYRA BECAME FED UP WITH BEING TREATED AS A BARREN WIFE...
YOU SAY YOU WANT A CHILD, BUT I SAY YOU DON'T, BECAUSE YOU HATE YOUR FATHER! BY NOT FATHERING A CHILD THAT WOULD BEAR HIS NAME, IT'S AS IF YOU WERE KILLING HIM!
PLEASE, DARLING! I'M NOT INTERESTED IN YOUR PSEUDO-PSYCHO-ANALYTIC THEORIES!
"...A BARREN WIFE WHOM, ACCORDING TO HEBRAIC TRADITION, I SHOULD HAVE REPUDIATED AFTER TEN YEARS, BUT WHOM I KEPT BY MY SIDE THROUGH SHEER COMPASSION...
YOU CAN SAY WHAT YOU WANT, "DARLING", BUT IT'S CRYSTAL-CLEAR THAT YOU'VE BEEN KILLING YOUR FATHER FOR A LONG TIME, LIKE WHEN, FOR OBSCURE REASONS, YOU CHANGED THE NAME HE GAVE YOU, MANGELOWSKI, INTO A COMMON MANGEL...
OF COURSE, MRS. FREUD, NEÉ LACAN!
TO HAVE A CHILD WOULD MEAN YOU'D BE-COME A FATHER, SOMETHING YOU'D DESPISE!
"TO GRANT WOMEN THE FREEDOM TO THINK IS LIKE PLACING A LOADED GUN INTO THE HANDS OF A CHILD."
"MYRA EVENTUALLY TOOK ME TO A FERTILITY SPECIALIST..."
DRIVE MORE CAREFULLY. I CAN'T READ!
YOU MALE CHAUVINIST PIG! I'M NOT YOUR SLAVE!
SARTRE VERITE ET EXISTENCE
JODO MOEB

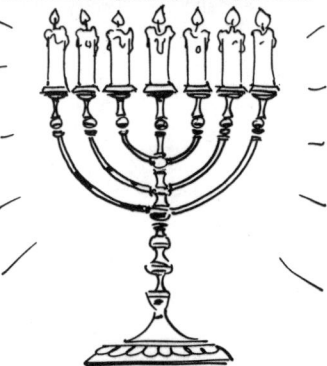

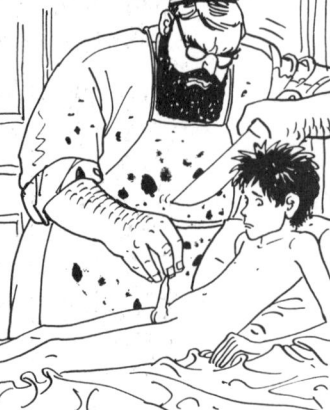

SO I SURRENDERED. I RETURNED TO JUDAISM BECAUSE IT IS THE WAY TO SANCTIFICATION. I ABANDONED WESTERN PHILOSOPHIES TO THROW MYSELF INTO TALMUDIC STUDIES...
BY BURYING MY INTELLECT, I OPENED MY HEART TO THE PROPHETIC WORD...
FROM THAT MOMENT ON, FOR ME, SEX LOST ALL ITS ANIMAL POWER, TO BECOME THE SOURCE OF A SACRED ENERGY...I BEGAN DRESSING IN PURPLE, THE COLOR OF SPIRITUAL RECEPTIVITY... AND I STOPPED HAVING ERECTIONS... AT LEAST, I THINK I DID...
BUT, ALAN, IT'S IMPOSSIBLE. YOU AREN'T...
NO, I'M NOT IMPOTENT, BUT I'VE MADE SEX A GIFT FROM MYSELF TO GOD! I'M NO LONGER A MAN, ELISABETH, BUT A PRIEST!
THAT IS WHY I ASK YOU FROM THE DEPTH OF MY SOUL TO HELP ME OVERCOME THE TEMPTATION THAT YOU REPRESENT FOR ME!
MOEB JODO

SALVATION ISN'T OBTAINED THROUGH SANITY, YOU SECOND-RATE PHILOSOPHER! YOUR "SANITY" IS A DEAD END, LEADING YOU TO YOUR DOOM! HEED MY WORDS, LITTLE MANGEL! INSANITY, DIVINE MADNESS, IS THE ONLY WAY TO SALVATION!
LET THE SEED OF LIFE GROW STRONG INSIDE YOU! LET YOUR SPERM CRAWL UP YOUR SPINE AND IRRIGATE YOUR BRAIN! LOOK AT THE WORLD THROUGH THE EYES OF A MADMAN!
DIVE INTO THE TORRID HEAT OF HER MOIST VULVA! ENJOY YOURSELF! COME! COME AT LAST!
LET HER BELIEVE THAT YOU'RE MAKING HER PREGNANT SINCE THAT IS WHAT SHE DESIRES!
I DON'T WANT TO HEAR ANYMORE! YOU'RE SCARING ME!
JODO MOEB

IT'S EXTRAORDINARY, PROF. MANGEL! YOU'RE AMAZINGLY LUCKY!
ME? WHY?
LABORATOIRE D'ANALYSES MED
BECAUSE THINGS LIKE THIS ONLY HAPPEN ONCE IN A MILLION CASES, IF THAT. YOU'VE BEEN SPONTANEOUSLY CURED. FOR NO APPARENT REASON, YOUR SPERM IS NOW NORMAL. LOOK, THEY'RE NO LONGER STUCK TOGETHER...
SO IT WAS ALL SOME KIND OF PSYCHOSOMATIC AFFLICTION?
ACCEPT IT AS A MIRACLE, MY LOVE.
IN ANY EVENT, THE DATES COINCIDE. YOU CAN CONSIDER YOURSELF THE FATHER OF THIS BEAUTIFUL, THREE-MONTH OLD FETUS. CONGRATULATIONS!
SO I'M GOING TO BE A FATHER AFTER ALL?
YES! OF A PROPHET!
CAREFUL! THERE'S A HOLE IN THE SIDEWALK!
DON'T OVERDO IT, ALAN! I'M PREGNANT, NOT HANDICAPPED!
THE NEW FURNITURE WILL BE HERE SOON, SO WE WON'T BE CAMPING FOR TOO MUCH LONGER. YOU KNOW I'M AGAINST ABORTION. BESIDES, THIS CHILD IS VERY IMPORTANT TO ME, SO I'LL TAKE CARE OF YOU...
THE CHILD'S IMPORTANT NOT ONLY TO YOU, ALAN, BUT FOR THE WHOLE OF MANKIND. YOU MUST LOOK THE TRUTH IN THE FACE!
NO! ENOUGH OF ALL THIS PSEUDO-CHRISTIAN MUMBO-JUMBO, ELISABETH! I'LL SEND YOU TO THE BEST ANALYST, AND HE'LL GET YOU BACK TO REALITY. YOU'RE JUST GOING THROUGH A PHASE OF MYSTIC DELUSIONS...
THAT'S WHERE YOU'RE WRONG, ALAN! YOU'RE CONFUSING DELUSIONS AND DIVINITY. MY CASE IS A LOT MORE COMPLEX THAN YOU THINK. LISTEN TO ME. NOT WITH YOUR MIND, BUT WITH YOUR HEART...
JODO MOEB 55

"WHEN YOU CAME BACK TO OUR HOTEL ROOM TO ASK FOR MY FORGIVENESS AND TO TELL ME YOU'D FELT YOU'D LET YOURSELF BE DRAGGED INTO MY 'DELUSIONS'..."

" THAT I COULD HARM YOUR REPUTATION, THAT YOU WOULDN'T SEE ME OR TALK TO ME AGAIN, AND WOULD EVEN BAR ME FROM ATTENDING YOUR LECTURES..."

" AFTER YOU'D FLED, SLINKING AWAY AFTER HAVING DEPOSITED FIVE THOUSAND FRANCS AT MY FEET, LIKE YOU'D BUY THE SILENCE OF A WHORE..."

"FOR THE FIRST FEW MINUTES, I WANTED TO DIE, BUT MY FAITH SOON OVERCAME MY DESPAIR. I KNEW I HAD TRIUMPHED, THAT GOD WAS WITH ME, AND I BE-GAN PRAYING WITH A RENEWED FERVOR..."

"THEN, I HAD A VISION, YES, A VISION, **NOT** A HALLUCINATION LIKE YOU THINK... I NEED NO PROOF, MY FAITH IS ENOUGH..."

"I SAW, FLOATING IN THE AIR, A HUMAN HEAD, WITH THE PEACEFUL EXPRESSION THAT ONLY THE DEAD HAVE...IT WAS JUST A HEAD, WITH AN INVISIBLE BODY..."

JODO MOEB SG

"I HEARD A VOICE THAT SAID: 'HAVE NO FEAR, ELISABETH! YOU HAVE NOT BEEN ABANDONED! THE HOLY GHOST IS WITH YOU. I AM SAINT JOSEPH! FIND ME AND I'LL TAKE YOU TO MARY!'"

"WHAT YOU DIDN'T KNOW WAS THAT, WHEN I SAW YOU AT THE SACRED-HEART, I WAS HOMELESS. TO CONCENTRATE ON MY STUDIES WITH YOU, I HAD QUIT MY JOB. WITH YOUR 5,000 FRS, I WAS ABLE TO STAY AT THE **AVENIR**."

"UNTIL I EVENTUALLY RAN OUT OF MONEY AND I HAD TO LEAVE. BUT I KNEW IT WOULDN'T MATTER, BECAUSE I WAS GOING TO FIND ST. JOSEPH, WHO WOULD HELP ME..."

"SOMETHING INSIDE TOLD ME TO GO TO THE SUBWAY STATION '**PYRAMIDS**,' AND THERE I CAME ACROSS A YOUNG ARAB WHOSE FACE WAS EXACTLY LIKE THE ONE I'D SEEN IN MY VISION!"

"HE IMMEDIATELY RECOGNIZED ME BECAUSE HE, TOO, HAD HAD A SIMILAR VISION! 'YOU'RE ELISABETH,' HE SAID, 'TAKE ME TO MARY,' I ASKED, 'AIN'T THE TIME YET; GOTTA WAIT THREE MONTHS. THEN, WE'LL NEED ZACHARIAS'S HELP TO FREE HER,' HE REPLIED..."

"MOUHAMAD-- ST. JOSEPH-- LIVED IN A MAID'S ROOM NEAR NOTRE-DAME. FOR THREE MONTHS, WE PRAYED EVERY DAY FOR YOU... AND FOR MARY!"

57

JODO MOEB

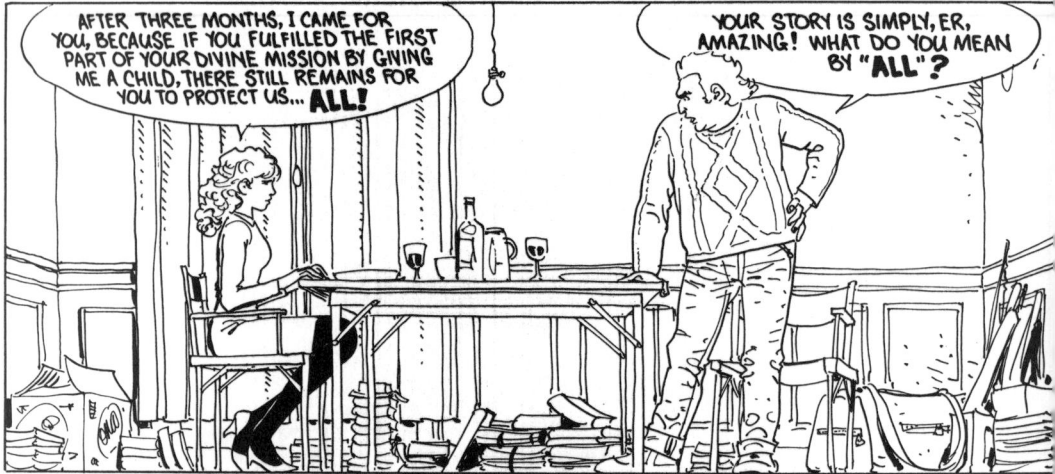

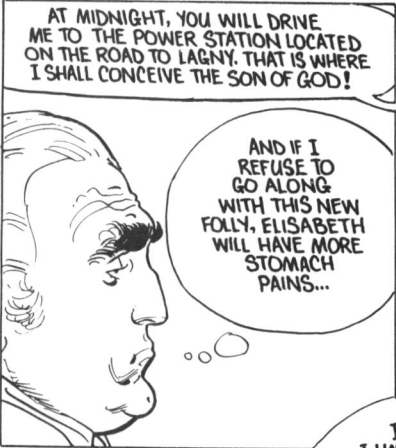

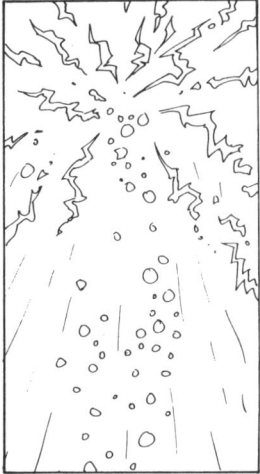

JODO MOEB 70

# CHAPTER TWO

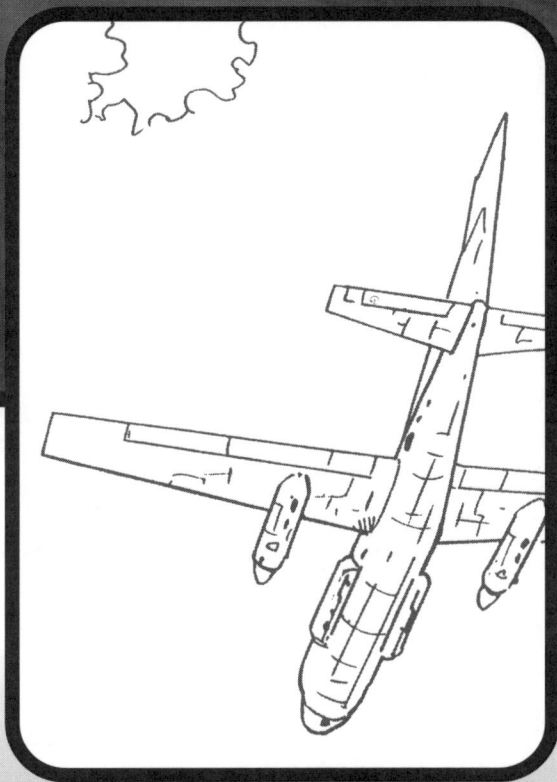

YOUR CYNICISM ASTOUNDS ME! EVEN THOUGH THE EVER-CHANGING CURRENTS OF LIFE ARE PULLING AT ME WITH UNSTOPPABLE POWER...

...I FORCE MYSELF TO BE IN LOVE, BECAUSE OTHERWISE I'D BE OVERWHELMED BY THE HORROR OF MY BEING. LIKE SARTRE, I BELIEVE THAT "TO EXIST IS TO DRINK OF ONESELF WITHOUT THIRST."

PFFFT!

BULL! YOU WANTED LOVE TO BRING YOU FREEDOM. INSTEAD, IT OPRESSES YOU. SUFFERING FROM LOVE IS YOUR OWN SLY WAY OF BEING HAPPY.

ME, HAPPY? YOU MUST BE JOKING! LOOK AT MY "FRIENDS" SPRAWLED ON THE BEACH, BASKING IN THE SUN, SHAMELESSLY WALLOWING IN THEIR MYSTICAL COSMOGONY.

THEY'RE THE ONLY FAMILY I'VE GOT LEFT.

THREE LUNATICS! YOU'RE IN DEEP SHIT, ALAN MANGEL. YOU, A DISTINGUISHED PROFESSOR OF PHILOSOPHY...

...AN AUTHORITY ON THE WRITINGS OF HUSSERL AND HEIDEGGER. HA! YOUR INSANE PASSION IS A REJECTION OF ALL THAT RESPECTABILITY!

TRUE! I'VE ALWAYS WANTED TO REJECT THAT WORLD, BUT I NEVER COULD BEFORE. NOW **IT** HAS REJECTED ME, AND IT'LL NEVER WELCOME ME BACK. **NEVER!**

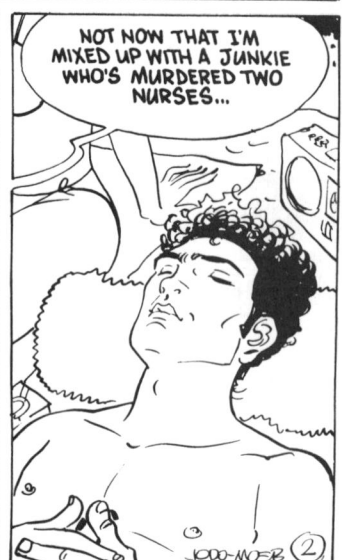

NOT NOW THAT I'M MIXED UP WITH A JUNKIE WHO'S MURDERED TWO NURSES...

JODO-MOEB ②

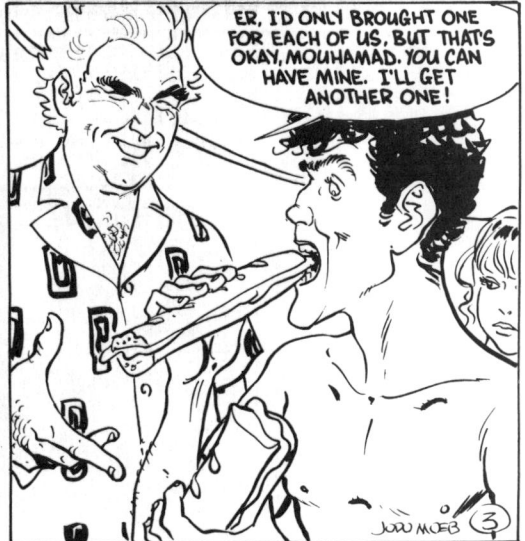

**Panel 1:** WOW!

COLIC AGAIN! IT MUST BE SERIOUS.

**Panel 2:** SLAM!

DON'T WORRY. I'LL TAKE CARE OF IT!

POOR BROTHER ZACHARIAS ...

**Panel 3:** TROUBLE MY PET?

YOU CAN SAY THAT AGAIN!

**Panel 4:** MY CREDIT CARD'S BEEN CANCELLED. I'M COMPLETELY BROKE. NO MONEY. NADA! MY BANK ACCOUNT IS AS DRY AS CARTESIAN TEXT!

**Panel 5:** YOU MADE ME SPEND ALL MY MONEY AS IF I WAS ROTHSCHILD. NOW WE'RE IN DEEP SHIT. IN DEEP SHIT!!

**Panel 6:** PPFRRTT GNAC! GNNINNNNNH

**Panel 7:** WE CAN'T AFFORD TO BUY FOOD OR PAY THE RENT ANYMORE. THEY'LL THROW US OUT OF THIS SHACK AND I WON'T EVEN BE ABLE TO BUY GAS FOR THE CAR. THE POLICE WILL ARREST US AND THEY'LL FIND OUT WE KILLED THOSE NURSES. AND EVEN IF THEY DON'T, WHAT ABOUT THE BABIES? HOW ARE WE GOING TO PAY THE DOCTORS? THE HOSPITAL? HOW?

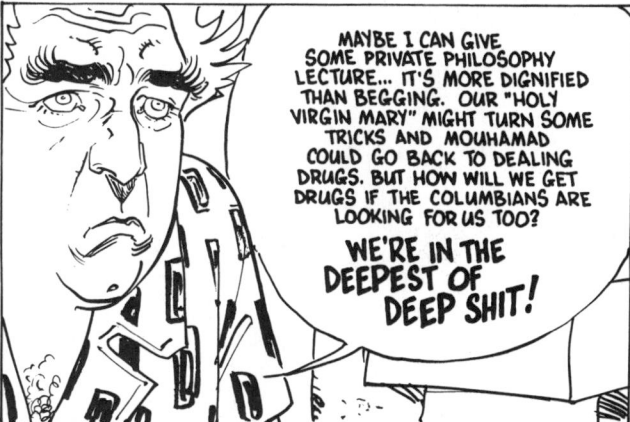

**Panel 8:** MAYBE I CAN GIVE SOME PRIVATE PHILOSOPHY LECTURE... IT'S MORE DIGNIFIED THAN BEGGING. OUR "HOLY VIRGIN MARY" MIGHT TURN SOME TRICKS AND MOUHAMAD COULD GO BACK TO DEALING DRUGS. BUT HOW WILL WE GET DRUGS IF THE COLUMBIANS ARE LOOKING FOR US TOO? WE'RE IN THE DEEPEST OF DEEP SHIT!

**Panel 9:** OOOUCHH!

PRRRT PLOUTCH FRT... FART

JODO MOEB ⑦

LISIEUX! A PLACE OF MIRACLES. AND THAT FIGURE--16--THE NUMBER OF THE TOWER ARCANA IN THE TAROT. GOD IS EVERYWHERE FOR THOSE WHO CAN SEE!
ER, YEAH, YEAH... STILL...
SHUT UP! YOUR "STILL" IS JUST ANOTHER "BUT." TO WIN, WE MUST BELIEVE WE SHALL WIN. LADY LUCK HAS BEEN SLEEPING UNTIL NOW, BUT WE'RE GOING TO AWAKEN HER!
WHAT'LL YOU HAVE?
ER, TWO GLASSES OF WATER.
YOU'RE GOING TO BET OUR LAST 100 FRANCS?
YOU BET! HA! HA! NOW CLEAR YOUR MIND OF ALL PROFANE THOUGHT AND PICK FIVE HORSES!
I CAN'T DO THAT, ELISABETH. I HAVE NO KNOWLEDGE OF HORSES!
WHICH ONES, ALAN?
1 AMBUSH BUG.
2 TIMOR OF MAREUIL.
3 VAGABOND KING.
4 UNAMORA.
5 CONGO REEF.
6 MASKED AVENGER.
7 TOOTSIE.
8 RIP-OFF ARTIST.
9 STYLGOR.
10 SELF-CONTROL.
11 ACTIVITY.
12 AURAVEA.
13 TIMORKY.
14 QUEEN L.
15 LUCKY BREAK.
16 VERMOUTH.
THIS IS TORTURE! THOSE NAMES MEAN NOTHING TO ME!
THE OPPOSITE OF A MIRACLE IS TO PRETEND NOT TO SEE. BE WILLING TO HEAL AND EVERYTHING YOU DESIRE WILL BE YOURS. VAGABOND KING, MASKED AVENGER, SELF-CONTROL, AURAVEA, AND LUCKY BREAK!
WHY THOSE FIVE?
VAGABOND KING: A POWER THAT CANNOT BE SHACKLED. AN ENLIGHTENED FOOL WHO CANNOT BECOME LOST SINCE ALL PATHS ARE HIS PATH. GOD IS SHOWING US THE WAY TO FREEDOM...
SELF-CONTROL: IF YOU CONTROL YOUR EGO AND SURRENDER YOURSELF TO GOD, THEN ALL CAN HAPPEN, BUT NOTHING BAD, FOR IN THE SACRED, THERE IS NO DANGER.
AURAVEA: RECEIVE THE DIVINE AURA IN YOUR BODY. MERGE YOUR SOUL WITH THE COSMOS. YOUR EGO KEEPS YOU ISOLATED, GOD REUNITES YOU...
JODO MOEB
11

MASKED AVENGER: YOU SEEK REVENGE CLOAKED IN ANONYMITY. BUT FROM WHAT? FROM NOT HAVING RECEIVED THE LOVE YOU DESIRED? IF YOU SECRETLY FORGIVE AND LOVE IN RETURN, THEN WILL THE LOVE YOU SEEK BE GIVEN TO YOU?

YOU GIVE ONLY WHAT YOU ARE, BUT IN EXCHANGE YOU WILL RECEIVE GOD FINALLY, LUCKY BREAK: HE WHO MAKES HIS OWN LUCK BY BREAKING HIS CHAINS AND RIDDING HIMSELF OF THE SHACKLES OF THE LACK OF FAITH.

ELISABETH! WHAT'S HAPPENING? HOW DID YOU COME UP WITH THIS? YOU SPEAK LIKE A PROPHET!

I HAVE NOTHING TO DO WITH THIS, ALAN. IT IS THE CHILD I'M BEARING WHO SPEAKS THROUGH ME!

SO DO WE BET OUR LAST FRANC OR NOT?

I YIELD TO YOUR INTOXICATING MADNESS. LET'S BET!

IF YOU DON'T MIND ME SAYING SO, SIR, MA'AM, YOU'VE PICKED THE WORST NAGS AROUND.

THERE'RE ONLY THREE FAVORITES IN THIS RACE: AMBUSH BUG, RIP-OFF ARTIST, AND VERMOUTH. THE OTHERS DON'T STAND A CHANCE.

I HAVE NO INTENTION OF DESCRIBING A SACRED EXPERIENCE, THE NATURE OF WHICH YOU COULDN'T POSSIBLY HOPE TO UNDERSTAND. JUST TAKE OUR BET.

THEY'VE LEFT THE GATE. LORD! I'M SO NERVOUS!

THEY'RE OFF!

DON'T BE AFRAID! GOD BELIEVES IN THOSE WHO SEEK HIM. IT IS HE WHO'LL MAKE US WIN!

GO, VERMOUTH!

JODO, MOEB. 12

# Panel 1

I'VE GOT A PAIN IN MY STOMACH! MY COLIC IS BACK!

STOP IT! YOU'RE GOING TO HAVE TO GET USED TO MIRACLES. **LOOK!**

BASTARDS!

**FIXED!**

CROOKS!

BOOOO!

BOOOOO!

# Panel 2

IT IS INDEED A DAY FOR SURPRISES! NOW RIPOFF ARTIST, NUMBER 8, LAST OF THE FAVORITES, IS BEING HELD BACK BY THE MAIN BODY OF RUNNERS...

?!

# Panel 3

...GIVING A UNIQUE OPPORTUNITY TO FIVE POORLY PLACED HORSES, VAGABOND KING, MASKED AVENGER, SELF-CONTROL...

IM-POSSIBLE!

# Panel 4

...AURAVEA, AND LUCKY BREAK, WHO'VE SPRUNG OUT LIKE ROCKETS AND PASSED EVERYONE ELSE!

GOOD LORD!

# Panel 5

INCREDI-I-IBLE BUT **TRUE!!** THOSE DARK HORSES HAVE JUST WON THE LISIEUX GRAND PRIX!!

# Panel 6

BOOOO! **CHEAT!!!**

MONEY BACK!

CROOKS!

INCREDIBLE!

INCREDIBLE INDEED.

IT'S... A MIRACLE!

ISN'T IT?

# Panel 7

HOW MUCH DID WE WIN, ANGEL OF MY HEART?

I DON'T KNOW THE EXACT FIGURE, BUT CONSIDERING THE ODDS... I'D SAY ABOUT THREE MILLION!

# Panel 8

TH-THREE M-MIL...

THREE MILLION FRANCS? *

# Panel 9

GASP!

?!

...

JODO MOEB 14

* ABOUT $600,000.

YOU AGAIN? YES, ME AGAIN!

I THOUGHT I WAS RID OF YOU FOR GOOD!

YEAH? YOU'LL NEVER CHANGE. YOU'RE STILL THE SAME SANCTIMONIOUS SUCKER. GOD, YOU'RE A PAIN. DON'T YOU REALIZE THAT YOU'VE JUST GOTTEN YOUR HANDS ON A FORTUNE? YOU ARE RICH, DO YOU HEAR ME, **RICH**!

WHAT HAS THAT GOT TO DO WITH YOU?

WHY ARE YOU HERE, TAKING THE CHANCE OF GETTING ARRESTED FOR STEALING A STUPID VIAL OF OIL? HAVE YOU FORGOTTEN YOU'RE ALREADY AN ACCESSORY IN THE MURDER OF TWO NURSES? BUY YOURSELF A ONE-WAY TICKET TO RIO AND VAMOOSE FOREVER. I'M TOLD THE LITTLE CHIQUITAS THERE HAVE THE BEST ASSES IN THE WORLD!

WILL YOU SHUT UP?

STOP TEMPTING ME! I'M MORE THAN SATISFIED SEXUALLY. ELISABETH IS EVERYTHING I COULD WISH FOR. I'M NOT LIKE YOU ANYMORE. I'M A MATURE, RESPONSIBLE ADULT, AND I WILL NOT ABANDON THE MOTHER OF MY CHILD!

?!?

SHE'S THE FIRST WOMAN I'VE EVER TRULY LOVED!

OK! OK! YOU LOVE HER. BUT DON'T BE STUPID ENOUGH TO **STEAL** THAT OIL-- ESPECIALLY **HERE**. BUY SOME IN A STORE. THEY'LL NEVER KNOW THE DIFFERENCE!

NO! I'VE LEARNED TO RESPECT THEIR MADNESS. I PROMISED TO BRING THEM BACK HOLY OIL FROM THE SACRED-HEART, AND THAT'S EXACTLY WHAT I'M GOING TO DO. NOW GO AWAY, YOU IMPUDENT GHOST! YOU MAKE ME SICK!

I TELL YA T' FUCK ME, YA BIG GALOOT!
ARF ARF!!
LEMME GO, YOU PUTRID OLD WOMAN!
AND YOU TOO, MANGY BASTARD! LET GO OF MY LEG!
ENOUGH!
TAKE THAT, YOU DISGUSTING DOG!
KAI!
DEAR GOD!
SEE WHERE COMPASSION GETS YOU? NOW YOU'VE KILLED HER. LET'S GET OUT OF HERE. THERE'S A PLANE FOR RIO LEAVING TONIGHT!
YOU AGAIN? GO AWAY, YOU IRRESPONSIBLE WRAITH!
THAT OLD WOMAN MAY ONLY BE HURT-- SERIOUSLY. I CAN'T ABANDON HER LIKE THAT!
WHY NOT? YOU'RE NOT GOING TO GO TO JAIL FOR A DRUNKEN OLD PERVERT, ARE YOU?
JODO MŒB
29

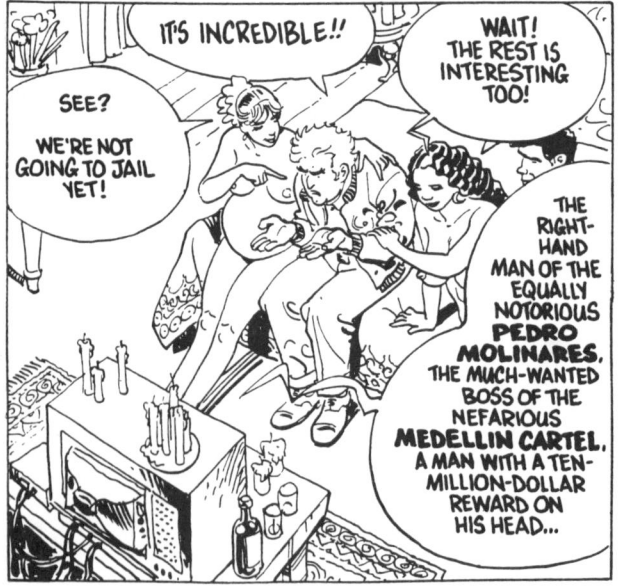

Panel 1: I TOLD YA T' WATCH 'ER LIKE TH' FUCKIN' APPLE OF YER FUCKIN' EYES, AND TH' DAY I COME T' GET 'ER OUTTA HERE, ALL THAT YA CAN TELL ME IS THAT SHE'S HIDIN' IN TH' FUCKIN' CLOSET?

NO, NO, MISTER LARA! I DIDN'T MEAN TO...

PLEASE UNDERSTAND. WE...

Panel 2: "I SAW THE GANGSTER PULL A STRANGE GUN FROM HIS JACKET..."

MISTER LARA!

PLEASE! NO! DON'T...

Panel 3: POLICE IDENTIFIED THE GUN AS AN ISRAELI M-22 LASER PISTOL-- A TOP-SECRET, EXPERIMENTAL GUN...

Panel 4: WHEN OUR ENEMIES FIND OUT SHE'S GONE, THEY'LL COME HERE T' ASK YA QUESTIONS. YER LOOSE ENDS, AND Y' KNOW WHAT HAPPENS T' LOOSE ENDS...

NO!

MERCY!

Panel 5: "IT'S JUST WHAT I TOLD YOU, BROS: TWO BEAMS OF LIGHT!"

ARGH! OOOOHW

"HE SHOT THEM IN COLD BLOOD. I SAW IT ALL. I'LL NEVER FORGET IT. IT WAS HORRIBLE!"

Panel 6: HOW DO YOU EXPLAIN THAT THE KILLER SPARED YOU, MR. DRUONT?

...TWO DEADLY BEAMS SENT BY THE GOD OF ISRAEL! D'YOU BELIEVE ME NOW, BROTHER ZACHARIAS?

ER...

I WAS TOTALLY PARALYZED, LIKE A VEGETABLE. IT SAVED MY LIFE!

Panel 7: AT LEAST ADMIT THAT YOUR FRIEND, SAINT JOSEPH AIN'T NO MURDERER!

OOOH, MOUHAMAD!

JODO MOEB 42

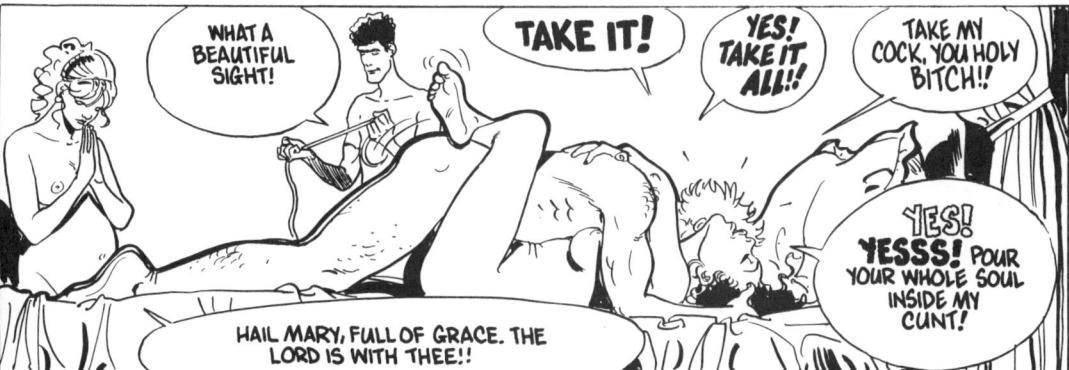

WHAT HAVE YOU DONE TO ME?!! I WAS A PROFESSOR AT THE SORBONNE, AN HONORABLE MAN. AND NOW WHAT AM I?
YES, TELL US: WHO ARE YOU?
I DON'T KNOW. IT'S AS IF... I'VE JUST BEEN BORN!
HALLELUJAH!
HALLELUJAH!
THE BAPTISM HAS BEEN CONSUMMATED!
HEY!! TAKE IT EASY! DON'T JOGGLE ME! MY ASS'S ON FIRE!!
WATCH OUT!
WHAT'S GOING...
?
!?
BAHOUM!
JODO MŒB
48

PUT YER HANDS UP, CABRON!
AIE!
BAM
RRATTATATATATAAAAAAA
PANGGG!
BANG!
?!
BBAAMM
PAW
PAW
BAW
PAW
BAM
RATATATATATATAAAA
PAW
TATATATAAAAAAAA
AIE!
CONO!! IT'S THE D·A·S·!!
GET DOWN AGAIN!!
MALDITO!
MUERAN BANDIDOS!
PAW
ARCH!
THEY WANT ME ALIVE. LIE DOWN BEHIND ME AND YOU'LL BE SAFE!
BEUARK!! IT SMELLS LIKE SHIT!!
SORRY, IT'S ME AGAIN. MY DAMN COLIC!
STAY CALM! EVERYTHING'S FINE!
COLUMBIAN SECRET SERVICE!
COME WITH US!
JODO MCEB
50

BLESSED ARE THE MARTYRS FOR THEIRS IS THE KING-DOM OF HEAVEN!
AMEN!
SAY YER LAST PRAYERS, FAGGOT!
NO!
PAW
ARRGH!
?
RRRATATATATATATT!!
PAW PAW
AARG!
HELP!
TERRO-RISTS!
ARGH!
POLICE!
SHOOT 'EM!
FIRE!
PAWW
RATARAATTATTATATATAATATATTTT
PAW
BOW
RATATTATRTATATATATATATATAA
DOM
DOOMMM
DAMN IT! IT'S THE GRINGOS FROM THE D·E·A·!
WE'VE GOT TO GET OUT OF HERE 'FORE THEY MOW US DOWN!
LORD, PROTECT MY SON, THY PROPHET!
JODO MOEB

I'M GONNA COUNT TO THREE...
AN' TRY TO FALL INTO THE WATER. WILLYA, MAC?
NO!
ONE...
JUST A SMALL MIRACLE. PLEASE...
oooTWOooo
ATATAT!
...THRARGH
TATATATAT
?
?
HA! HA! HA! HA!
DIE GRINGOS CABRONES!
RATATATATATATATATAH
TATATATATATAAHHHH
?!
AIE!
OUCH!
ARGH!
PAMM PAW
?!
SHIT!
JODO MOEB
55

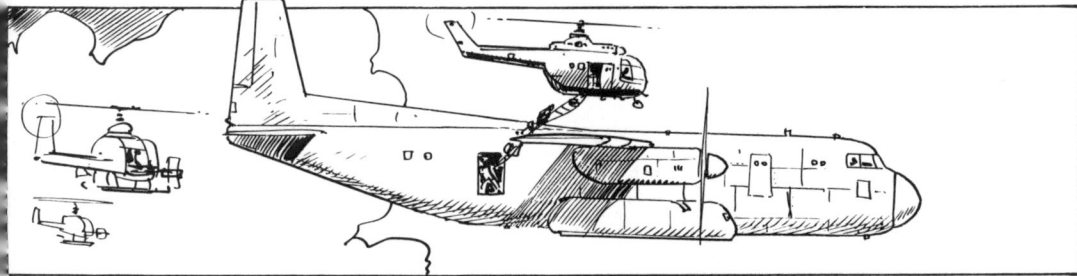

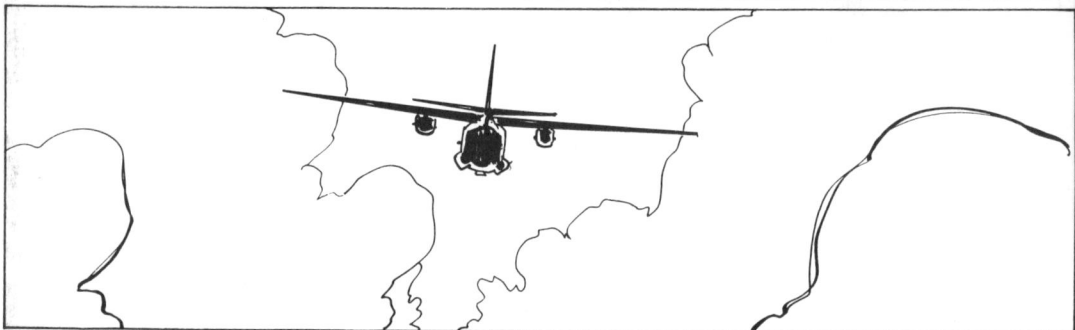

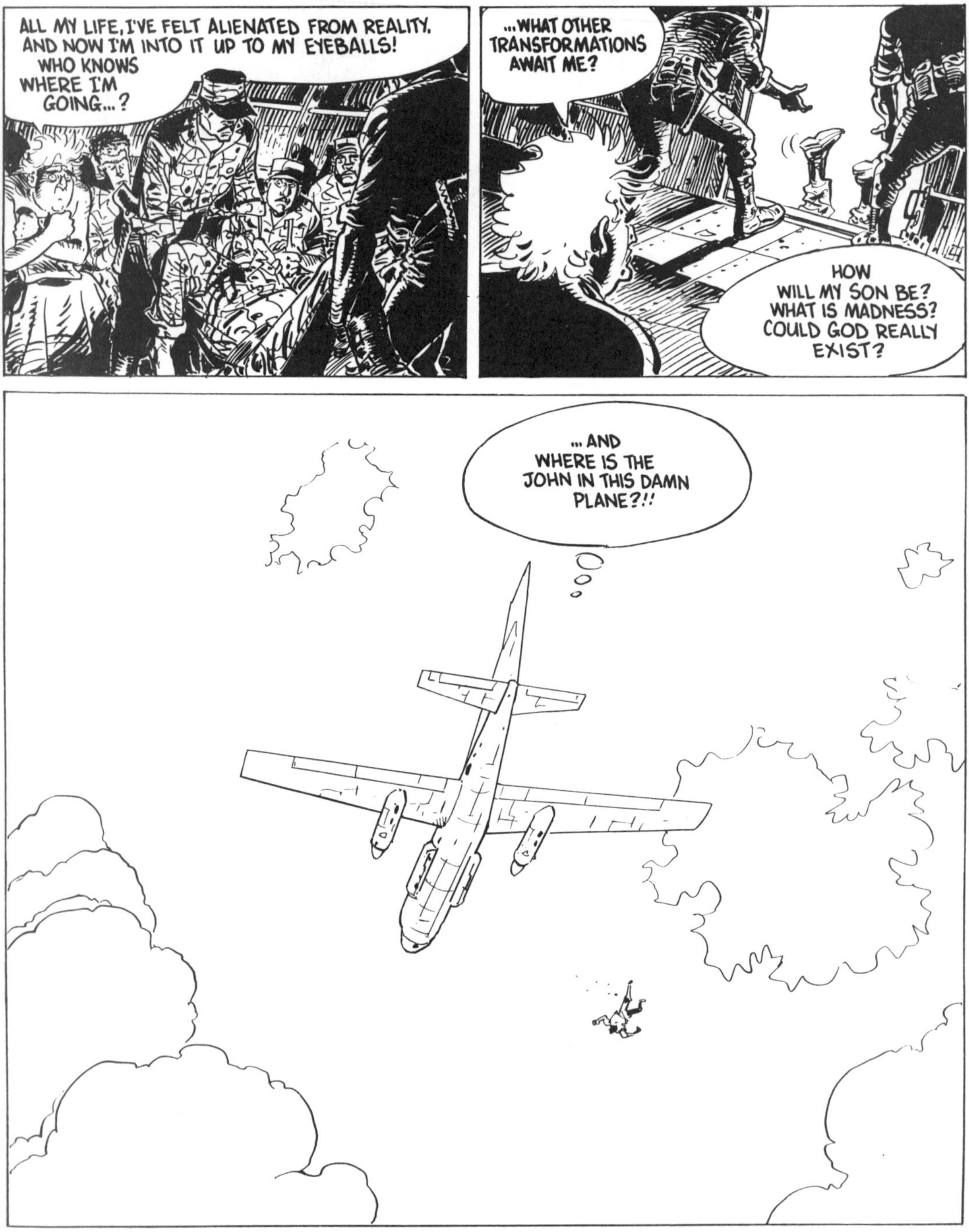


THE END (FOR NOW)?

ALEXANDRO JODOROWSKY was born in Chile in 1930. His father's father had fled persecution as a Jew in Russia to open a South American shoe factory, and his mother was the daughter of a Russian ballet dancer. Young Alexandro was precocious; by the age of four, he'd learned to read and was soon seduced by the swashbuckling world of French pulp literature, devouring novels like *The Three Musketeers* and *The Count of Monte Cristo*.

In 1942, Jodorowsky's family moved to Santiago, where he attended school. While majoring in philosophy and psychology at the University of Santiago, he worked as a circus clown and eventually left school to pursue a career in the theater.

Jodorowsky moved to Paris in 1955, where he studied for six years under Marcel Marceau, writing a number of plays for the master mime. During this time, he directed the legendary Maurice Chevalier in a one-man show at the Alhambra Theater.

Jodorowsky fell in with a group of Parisian artists who shared an interest in spiritual matters, surrealism, new-age philosophies, and art. These friends included Spanish filmmaker Fernando Arrabal and cartoonist Roland Topor. In 1962, the three men created a cultural movement called "Panic," in honor of the Greek god Pan. This was meant to include everything the surrealists embraced, plus a number of things they rejected, including pop art, science fiction, comics, and rock music.

He left the Paris art scene after helping Arrabal and Topor stage a four-hour "happening" at the American Cultural Center, during which Arrabal danced to *Swan Lake* while pouring ground meat on broken glass. In 1965, Jodorowsky resettled in Mexico.

In 1970, Jodorowsky wrote, directed, and starred in *El Topo*, his second film. The mix of mysticism with a traditional western caught the attention of Andy Warhol and Mick Jagger. Various critics made comparisons to Bergman's *Seventh Seal* and Browning's *Freaks*, Sergio Leone and Sam Peckinpah, and Jesus and Buddha.

After a third film, *The Holy Mountain*, Jodorowsky began work on an adaptation of Frank Herbert's *Dune*, bringing together H.R. Giger, Moebius, and Dan O'Bannon to create the look of the various worlds. The project proved too expensive for its backers and was abandoned after two years of hard work. O'Bannon went on to work with Giger and Moebius on *Alien*, directed by Ridley Scott.

In 1978, Jodorowsky and Moebius collaborated on the short, eerie masterpiece, "The Eyes of the Cat." Jodorowsky has continued to write for comics, including *The Incal* with Moebius, *Alef-Thau* with Arno, and *The Saga of the Meta-Baron* with Juan Giminez. His later film work includes *The Rainbow Thief* and *Santa Sangre*.

JEAN GIRAUD, a.k.a. MOEBIUS, was born on May 8, 1938 near Paris. From an early age he showed great interest and talent in illustration, leading him to attend the School of Applied Arts. In 1954, still in school, he wrote and drew his first western strip, *Franck and Jeremie*, thereby launching a career as a prominent western artist.

After being discharged from the army in 1960, Giraud assisted the famous Belgian artist Joseph Gillain ("Jije") on his *Jerry Spring* western series, later doing illustrations for a series of encyclopedia-like books for Hachette. It is at that time that Giraud started using the Moebius signature on his more dark-humored comic strips in the satirical magazine *Hari-Kiri*.

After a stint of illustrating French science-fiction books and magazines, Moebius returned to comics and in 1975 co-founded *Metal Hurlant*. His work of this period, including *Arzach* and *The Airtight Garage*, became very influential on comics artists worldwide, aided in part by the birth of *Heavy Metal* (1977), translating and reprinting his work and others for an American audience.

The attention led to a new direction in Moebius's career as a design conceptualist for the motion-picture industry. After Jodorowsky's failed *Dune* project,

Moebius went on to work on such films as Ridley Scott's *Alien*, René Laloux's *The Time Masters*, Disney's *Tron*, George Lucas's production of *Willow*, and James Cameron's *The Abyss*, as well as contributing designs to Euro-Disney.

In the eighties, a great body of his work was reprinted by Marvel Comics in the United States, for whom he drew a special *Silver Surfer* comic in 1988. Besides this comics and film work, Moebius has kept busy as one of Europe's top commercial artists. He's done book covers for Kurt Vonnegut and Harlan Ellison, magazine covers for *Glamour*, *L'Express*, and *Le Monde*, and album covers for Guy Beart and Jimi Hendrix, as well as ad campaigns for Greenpeace, Citroen, and Maxwell House.

His original art has hung in France, Austria, Belgium, Canada, Italy, Mexico, and the United States. French Minister of Culture Jack Lang, in 1985, consecrated him Best Artist in Graphic Arts, and President Mitterand named him Knight of Arts and Letters, the highest French decoration for cultural and artistic achievements. A postage stamp honoring him and bearing one of his designs was issued by the French government in 1988.

Jean "Moebius" Giraud now resides in Paris.

# SCIENCE-FICTION/FANTASY BOOKS AVAILABLE FROM DARK HORSE COMICS

## MOEBIUS
**ARZACH**
Moebius
80-page color paperback
ISBN: 1-56971-132-1 $6.95

**THE MAN FROM THE CIGURI**
Moebius
80-page color paperback
ISBN: 1-56971-135-6 $7.95

## THE BOOK OF NIGHT
Vess
112-page color/B&W paperback
ISBN: 1-878574-25-6 $12.95

## CONCRETE
**KILLER SMILE**
Chadwick
144-page color paperback
ISBN: 1-56971-080-5 $16.95

## DOMU
**A CHILD'S DREAM**
Otomo
240-page B&W paperback
ISBN: 1-56971-140-2 $17.95

## HARLAN ELLISON'S DREAM CORRIDOR
Ellison & Various
64-page color paperback
ISBN: 1-56971-084-8 $4.95

## KLING KLANG KLATCH
McDonald • Lyttleton
80-page color paperback
ISBN: 1-878574-41-8 $11.95

## THE LEGEND OF MOTHER SARAH
**TUNNEL TOWN**
Otomo • Nagayasu
224-page B&W paperback
ISBN: 1-56971-145-3 $18.95

## THE LUCK IN THE HEAD
Harrison • Miller
80-page color paperback
ISBN: 1-878574-46-9 $11.95

## STAR WARS
**DARK EMPIRE**
Veitch • Kennedy
184-page color paperback
ISBN: 1-56971-073-2 $17.95

**DARK EMPIRE II**
Veitch • Kennedy
168-page color paperback
ISBN: 1-56971-119-4 $17.95

## Available from your local comics retailer!